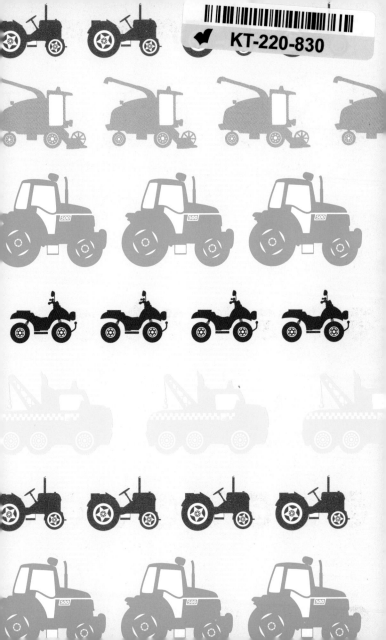

KT-220-830

A catalogue record for this book is available from the British Library

© 2005 Little Entertainment Company Limited/Entertainment Rights PLC. All Rights Reserved.
Adapted from the television script by Keith Littler, based on the original stories by Colin Reader.
Photographs by James Lampard.

Published by Ladybird Books Ltd.
A Penguin Company
80 Strand London WC2R 0RL

4 6 8 10 9 7 5 3

LADYBIRD and the device of a ladybird are trademarks of Ladybird Books Ltd.
All rights reserved. No part of this publication may be reproduced,
stored in a retrieval system, or transmitted in any form or by any means,
electronic, mechanical, photocopying, recording or otherwise,
without the prior consent of the copyright owner.

ISBN-13: 978-1-84422-697-9
ISBN-10: 1-8442-2697-2

Printed in Italy

Circles In
The Corn

One morning, Stan was busy tinkering with Little Red Tractor's engine while he listened to the radio.

"Tonight's film in the park, 'Rockets from Outer Space', has sold out," said the DJ.

"That's a shame," sighed Stan, "I like science fiction films."

He tightened one last bolt.

"That's you done Little Red Tractor," he said. "We'd better see if our corn is ready for harvesting – let's go!"

"Toot! Toot!" piped Little Red Tractor, happily raising the lid on his exhaust pipe.

Mr Jones and Big Blue sat in Beech
Farm's Upper Field, looking at their
golden crop.

  "Looks like our corn is almost ready,"
grinned Mr Jones. But then... zzzzzzZZZ!
A wasp started to circle Mr Jones' head.

"Buzz off!" snapped Mr Jones. "We'll come back tomorrow Big Blue."

But before Big Blue could move, the wasp was at it again.

"Go away!" Mr Jones shouted. His foot slipped off the clutch, plunging Big Blue into the cornfield.

Big Blue went crashing through the field, making crazy circles in the corn.

"Ouch, that hurts!" cried Mr Jones, as the wasp stung him on the bottom! He slammed on the brakes just before Big Blue hit a wall.

"Oh my, that was close," puffed
Mr Jones.

"Honk! Honk!" agreed Big Blue.

"We'll do the harvesting now,"
Mr Jones said. "I don't want anyone
to see this mess."

The pair went to fetch Harvey the
combine harvester.

Mr Jones rushed back with Harvey, but Big Blue's crazy circles had already been seen.

"It's that dratted reporter," Mr Jones scowled.

Skip Shutter was leaning over the gate, taking photographs.

"Did you see what happened?"
Skip asked.

"Erm, I... found it like this this
morning," stuttered Mr Jones. "It
must have been ramblers."

"Nonsense!" replied Skip. "It's
space rockets!"

"It's the only answer," Skip continued. "They land at night and make these wonderful patterns."

"But…" stuttered Mr Jones.

"People will pay to see this," beamed the reporter.

"Money?" gasped Mr Jones.

"Yes! This really is a scoop," Skip said, getting excited. "I'll be the talk of the town."

While the reporter rambled on about headlines and flying saucers, Mr Jones started to think…

Stan arrived at Beech Farm. He'd come to borrow Harvey, but Big Blue was parked alone.

"Mr Jones must be harvesting," Stan said to Little Red Tractor. "How about we go home and give you a polish?"

At the yard, Stan put on the radio.

"For a small fee you'll see corn circles made by space rockets," said a familiar voice – Mr Jones'!

"What is Mr Jones up to?" chuckled Stan. "We can't miss this!"

The lane beside Upper Field had been transformed. Ryan and Amy were standing on a viewing platform and there was a long queue.

"I can't believe it," whispered Ryan.

"The rocket must have been huge," added Amy.

"So what's this about space rockets?" asked Stan as he and Little Red Tractor arrived.

"Fifty pence please," said Mr Jones.

Stan peered into the field. "They look like tractor tracks to me."

"These are rocket tracks," announced Skip, "and they will be back."

Mr Jones looked up with a start.

"They happen in twos. There'll be even bigger tracks in the fields by morning," Skip went on.

Mr Jones gulped. What had he got himself into?

Standing behind them, Walter had overheard everything. This could be his big chance to see a real UFO!

"I can't make the film tonight Nicola," he said.

His daughter looked disappointed.

"I'll come with you," offered Stan.

"That would be great," smiled Nicola.

When it was dark, Walter made his way to Upper Field.

"This is it," he chuckled. "A chance to see a rocket from outer space."

But someone had got there first… Skip Shutter!

"Come over here," whispered the reporter.

While Walter and Skip kept watch, Stan and Little Red Tractor were driving home from the movie.

"That was great," said Stan. "Although the rockets were a bit far-fetched."

"Toot! Toot!" parped Little Red Tractor. He didn't get to see a film very often.

Walter and Skip were happily eating cheese and cucumber sandwiches, when something strange started to happen.

"The earth is shaking," noticed Skip. "And that noise…"

A loud rumble was coming from the top of the cornfield.

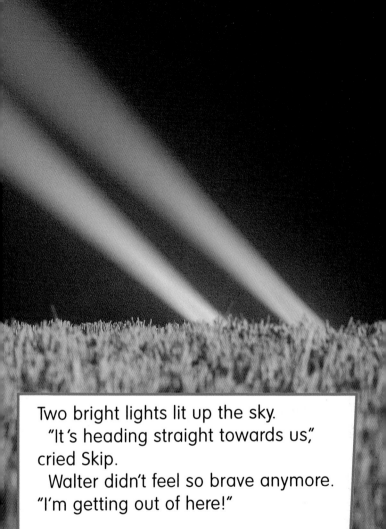

Two bright lights lit up the sky.
  "It's heading straight towards us,"
cried Skip.
  Walter didn't feel so brave anymore.
"I'm getting out of here!"

Stan noticed two shapes jumping about on Mr Jones' land.

"What's that?" he asked Little Red Tractor.

A bright beam suddenly flashed overhead, lighting up Walter and Skip. Stan and Little Red Tractor raced towards Upper Field.

When they arrived, the UFO-spotters
were in a terrible pickle.

  "Save me!" wept Skip, jumping into
Walter's arms. The beams of light
were getting closer and closer.

  "Look out!" cried Stan, and Little Red
Tractor tooted with all his might to
warn the circling lights that there
were people ahead.

Big Blue, not a space rocket, came to a halt in front of them.

"Who's there?" asked a small voice.

"Mr Jones?" asked Walter.

"So you made the circles!" said Skip.

"This is all your fault," Mr Jones answered crossly.

"The main thing is that everyone is okay," said Stan.

"Thanks to Little Red Tractor," nodded Walter.

"THAT'S my big story!" cried Skip. "Rocket enthusiasts saved by brave tractor."

Stan proudly patted Little Red Tractor.

"Toot! Toot!" Little Red Tractor beeped happily.